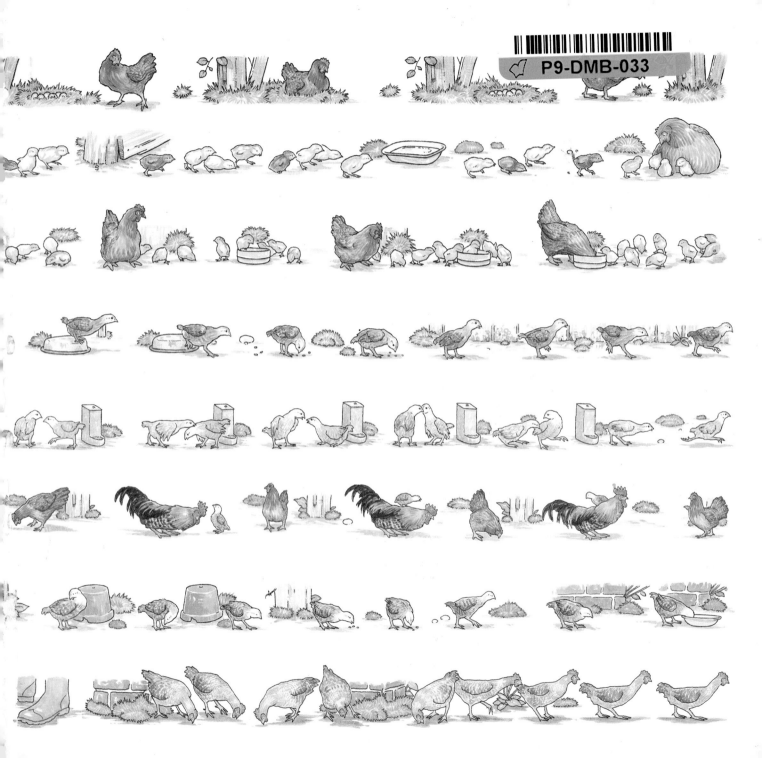

Library of Congress Cataloging-in-Publication Data

Burton, Jane.
  Chick/photographed by Jane Burton.—1st American ed.
  p. cm.—(See how they grow)
  Summary: Photographs and text depict the development of a chick
from the egg stage to the eighth week.
  ISBN 0-525-67355-5
  1. Chicks—Juvenile literature. 2. Chickens—Development—
Juvenile literature. [1. Chickens. 2. Animals—Infancy.]
I. Title. II. Series.
SF487.5.B874 1991
598'.617—dc20   91–96
                                                                CIP
                                                                AC

First published in the United States in 1992 by Lodestar Books,
an affiliate of Dutton Children's Books, a division of
Penguin Books USA Inc.
375 Hudson Street,
New York, N.Y.10014

Originally published in Great Britain in 1991 by
Dorling Kindersley Limited, 9 Henrietta Street, London WC2E 8PS

Printed in Italy by L.E.G.O.   ISBN 0–525–67355–5
First American Edition   10 9 8 7 6 5 4 3 2 1

Written by Angela Royston
Editor Mary Ling
Art Editor Nigel Hazle
Production Marguerite Fenn
Illustrator Rowan Clifford

Color reproduction by Scantrans, Singapore

SEE HOW THEY GROW

CHICK

photographed by
JANE BURTON

Lodestar Books • Dutton • New York

Hatching

This is my mother. She is sitting on her eggs. Inside each egg a chick is growing. One of them is me.

I start to chip around the inside of my eggshell.

I push my shell apart.

At last I am free.

Out of the egg

I am one hour old. My brothers
and sisters have
hatched too.
We are
chirping to
each other.

My feathers have dried,
and now they are soft
and downy.

Learning to feed

I am three days old, and I am feeling
hungry. My mother is eating seed.
How does she do it?
I watch her
carefully.

I stretch
up and take the seed
from her beak.

It tastes so good
I decide to peck
some myself.

A drink of water

I am eight days old now. New feathers are growing on my wings.

What is Mom doing? She is dipping her beak into a bowl of water.

I hop into the bowl.
The water is cool and wet.
My sister is getting in too.

False alarm

I am two weeks old.
Today I am looking
for food with
my mother.

Is something wrong?
My mother is flapping
her wings.
She clucks
at us to run
away.

It is a false alarm.
Nothing is wrong.
Mother calls us
back.

Meeting Dad

I am four weeks old now. I am growing bigger every day.

Here is my father.
Look how big he is!

Dad is very friendly.
He lets me ride on
his back.

Growing bigger

I am eight weeks old,
and all my feathers have
grown.

I have a
bright red
comb on
my head and a
red wattle under my beak.

I am big and strong. At last I can look after myself.

I use my beak to keep myself clean and tidy. I am proud of my fine feathers.

See how I grew

The egg

One hour old

Three days old

Eight days old

Two weeks old

Four weeks old   Eight weeks old

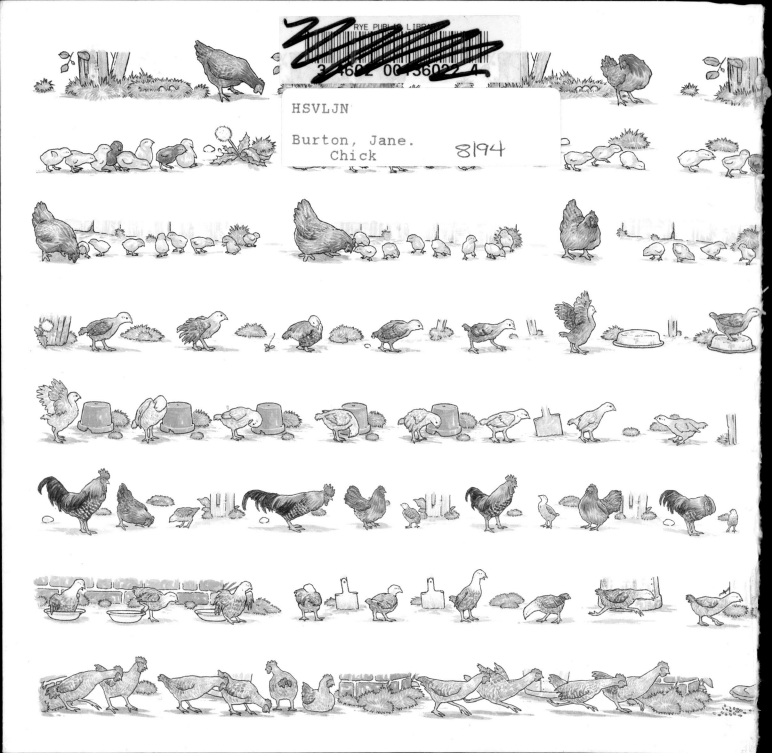